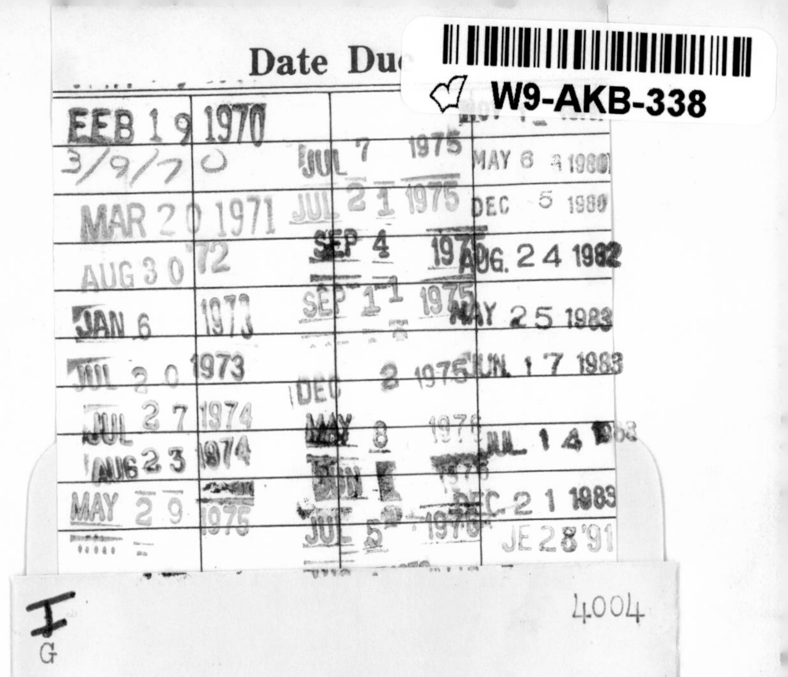

Groves-Raines, Antony
The tidy hen

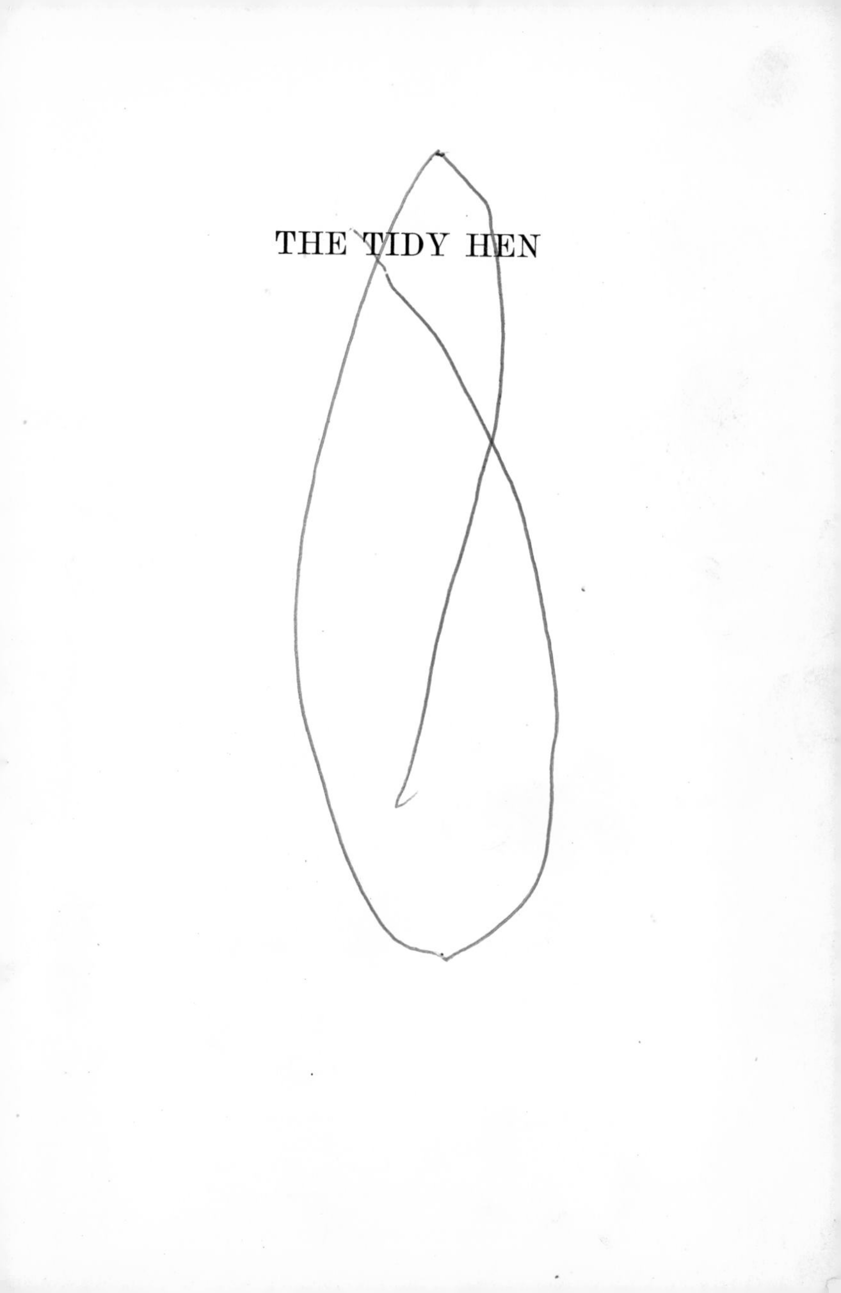

THE TIDY HEN

also illustrated by Antony Groves-Raines

ON CHRISTMAS DAY IN THE MORNING!

THE TIDY HEN

ANTONY GROVES-RAINES

HARCOURT, BRACE & WORLD, INC., NEW YORK

To Julia and Nannie

First edition
Library of Congress Catalog Card Number: 61-6116
Printed in the United States of America

THE TIDY HEN

Every morning, when the henhouse door was opened, the hens came running out for a drink of water. The first at the trough was always a big, bold, bossy hen who would stand for no nonsense from anybody. Until *she* had finished drinking (and what a long time she took), no other hen would dare to take a sip for fear of getting a good sharp peck on the head. Next at the trough was a spiteful, fluttery hen with a long, yellow beak, and she certainly knew how to use it. The others had to wait until she, too, had drunk her fill, for she would peck them too—all but old Madam Bossy. So it went on from highest to lowest until last of all there would come hurrying from the henhouse a small black hen called Olga, with a feather duster in her beak. *Everybody* pecked Olga; she was the most henpecked hen in the whole yard!

When the other hens got up in the morning, Olga had to go round with her feather duster, dusting the perches and tidying up the nests for the day's laying. Everything had to be as neat as ninepence before Olga was allowed her morning drink of water.

Olga grew very tired of work, work, work and never a word of thanks, let alone wages. She often thought of leaving the yard and taking a job elsewhere, but it is difficult for a hen.

One day when Olga was scratching around under the kitchen window, she overheard Cook speaking angrily to the little girl who lived in the house.

"What's this coat doing, lying on the floor?" she was saying. "And here's an odd slipper under the chair and, mercy me, if that isn't one of your good hair ribbons lying in the coal scuttle! I declare there never was a more untidy girl! I'm sick and tired of tidying up after you. You can just go out and hire yourself a personal maid!"

Olga was most interested in what she heard. Perhaps this was a job for her! Surely even a little girl couldn't be as untidy as two dozen hens. A moment later the back door opened and Julia, for that was the little girl's name, wandered gloomily out, forgetting of course to shut the door behind her. Olga slipped inside. She would

tidy up, just to show Julia what an excellent personal maid she could be.

Around the door she scuttled, and from then on it was easy to find her way up to Julia's room. She just followed a trail of dropped handkerchiefs, candy papers, a bedroom slipper, socks (one blue and one white), and a sweater. And the door into Julia's room was open.

Once inside the room, the problem was where to begin; it looked as though a small tornado had swept in through the window. Olga noticed a pretty little white apron in a jumble of dresses in the dolls' cupboard and put it on. With her neat, black plumage and her feather duster she felt very smart and professional.

Then she decided to tidy up the shoes that lay scattered about. The slippers were fairly easy, but a pair of outdoor shoes was too heavy to drag, so Olga had to sit in each one and paddle herself across the room with her feet. Finally she got them all arranged in a neat row under the wardrobe.

Next there was a straw hat to be put away on a top shelf, which was *very* difficult. In the end she nestled down inside it, clutching tightly with her claws, and flapped her wings wildly until she rose in the air. But she had to make a pancake landing, and the hat was rather squashed.

Socks and other odds and ends were quite simple, especially as one drawer was open. Olga popped everything inside, including part of an apple and a slightly sucked caramel that Julia was saving for later.

With her feather duster Olga then swept

up little bits of straw and orange seeds and some candy papers and other remnants. She made a neat pile of it all and brushed it under the carpet.

Now it was time to do a little sewing, for Olga had noticed several buttons missing from some of the clothes. She jumped onto the dressing table to get the workbasket, and there, looking at her out of the mirror, was another black hen!

Olga took a step toward the other hen just to tell her, quite politely of course, that she must have made a mistake about the room. But the other hen advanced too, ruffling up her feathers and glowering most ferociously, so that Olga had to give her one good sharp peck on the head, in order to teach that hen to mind her manners.

Well, goodness knows what that hen's head was made of! Whatever it was, it nearly knocked poor Olga out.

When she had recovered, she pushed the workbasket as far as possible away from the mirror and took out a needle and thread and the button box. Some of the buttons glittered and looked rather attractive. Olga, who was feeling hungry after her experience, tried a few. They hadn't much taste, really, but were not disagreeable.

She threaded the needle by sticking it upright in the pincushion and running at it.

The buttons got sewn on somehow, one stitch per button and a knot at the back, but the scissors were hard to manage.

And in the end the buttons weren't all of the same size.

Nor were they *exactly* of the same color.

Olga happened to notice that some of the dolls' dresses were very dirty. So she collected them and carried them into the bathroom. It was a bit awkward for her to turn on the water with her feet, but she managed it, though the basin got rather more full than she had intended. There was a tricky moment when Olga really thought she would have to cackle for help.

Then she dropped in the dolls' clothes and added some soap flakes. This took a long time, as she had to put in the soap flakes beakful by beakful, for the box was too big to handle. And a beakful of soap flakes is certainly a very disagreeable thing.

By then she began to wish that a duck had been hired to do the laundry because the only way she could wash the clothes was by getting into the water and stamping up and down. It was a horrid experience, for the more she stamped, the fluffier became the soap flakes, until all that could be seen of Olga was her head, peeping out of a mountain of suds. She was very glad indeed to pull out the stopper, but even then it took ages to get the suds to run away, and they stuck all over poor Olga so that she looked like a meringue on legs.

Twilight had come by the time her feathers were dry, and then she had to turn back the quilt on Julia's bed. This took quite a while, with a lot of flying backwards and forwards, before it was neatly folded, and Olga, after her busy day, began to feel very tired indeed. The bed looked so cozy that

SOAP
FLAKES

she just couldn't help settling down for a rest.

And before she knew where she was she had laid an egg!

At that moment there was a sound of footsteps on the stairs, and Olga, feeling shy and nervous, just had time to fly to the top of the wardrobe before Julia came in.

The little girl slowly undressed, put on her night things, and brushed her teeth in the bathroom. Then, with a yawn and a stretch, she jumped into bed....

CRUNCH! SQUELCH!

It was the most HORRIBLE feeling!!

Poor Julia let out a yell, and Cook came hurrying up the stairs, crying:

"Whatever is the matter?"

There was egg EVERYWHERE.

All over the sheets, all over the pillow-case; it was *disgusting!*

"Oh my, oh my, oh my!" cried Cook. "Everything will have to be changed. Now, whatever were you doing with an egg in your bed?"

Julia continued to wail, but Cook suddenly caught sight of Olga, peering anxiously over the top of the wardrobe.

"I declare to goodness!" she exclaimed. "Fancy keeping a hen in your bedroom!"

"I didn't," sobbed Julia.

"Well, there'll be no more hens in this house, and that's a fact!"

And Cook bundled poor Olga down the stairs and out the back door.

So there she was, out of a job, darkness coming on, and the henhouse shut up. Not that she wanted to go back to those nasty, selfish hens who always grabbed the best perches, but it wasn't very pleasant to be alone out there with the thought of foxes at the back of her mind.

And then it began to rain.

Olga hurried over to the cart shed. She really didn't feel safe on the ground, so she fluttered and scrambled up the side of the cart until she found herself a wobbly perch on the chain that hangs between the shafts.

It wasn't comfortable and it was *very* drafty, but at least it was high up, out of the way of things that prowl in the night.

What a night! The rain poured down. The wind whistled and swirled through the cart shed, rocking poor Olga on her perch so that she had to cling like a clothespin.

And when the wind died down, the shed was filled with rustlings and scuttlings, and there was even a certain amount of sniffing around the wheels of the cart. Olga froze on her perch and kept her eyes tightly shut, for she couldn't bear to look.

At last the sun came up and the henhouse door was opened. By then Olga was thankful to see the hens come tearing out into the sunlight, and she flew down in her white

apron to join them. The lesser hens were respectfully awaiting their turns at the trough, and old Madam Bossy was about to have her morning drink. Suddenly, she caught sight of Olga fluttering toward them. Never in her life had she seen a hen in an apron! She gave one squawk and fled, just as though Olga were the Hen from Mars. The other hens, when they saw the behavior of Madam Bossy, scattered in every direction, cackling their heads off, so that Olga had the water trough all to herself, and she took her time over it.

And after that Olga never had trouble again. She only had to give a hen *one look* to make her mind her P's and Q's. And on washing day Olga always rinsed out her apron under the tap of the rain-water barrel and hung it on the line to dry so that it was spotlessly white and fresh.

But every morning, *after* her drink at the water trough, Olga still dusted the hen-house with her feather duster because, although she didn't *have* to do it, she was the sort of hen who likes to keep things as neat and tidy as a NEW PIN.